Rucker
The Lost Country Dog

Make Your Mark Publishing, LLC, Atlanta, GA

Cover design by Connie M. Huddleston
Cover photo by Gittel C. Price

Printing History: July 2012

Library of Congress Cataloging-in-Publication Data
DeNiro, Elaine, Rucker, The Lost Country Dog, Author/Elaine DeNiro
p.
ISBN 978-0-9839660-4-3

1.Children's Fiction
2.Dogs
3.Georgia
4.Georgia History

2012941570
Printed in the United States of America

RUCKER
THE LOST COUNTRY DOG

By
Elaine DeNiro

Proceeds from the sale of this book benefit
the Roswell Historical Society,
a non-profit organization dedicated
to the preservation of the history of Roswell, Georgia.

Rucker was a country dog who lived on a farm with the Stewart family. Rucker loved taking naps in the front yard of his farmhouse, chasing chickens in the barnyard, and playing fetch with his owners in the cotton fields. He was a very happy country dog. Rucker had never been to the nearby town of Roswell before and had always wondered what it was like.

Two of the Stewart boys worked at a sawmill near their farmhouse. Rucker went to the sawmill every day and waited patiently outside for Walter and Derrell to finish work. One day, the boys left work early. They needed to pick up some buttons and ribbons for their mother at Roswell's General Store. "Go home, Rucker," said Walter. "We'll be back later." Rucker knew he should listen to the boys, but he couldn't help but think, "This is my chance to see the town!" He jumped into the back of the wagon when the boys weren't looking and hid under a burlap sack.

After a long and bumpy ride, the wagon arrived in town and stopped in front of the General Store. The boys went inside to get the buttons and ribbons their mother needed. Rucker peeked out from under the sack and was excited to see the town all around him. Now Rucker was a curious dog, and he wanted to see all the sights, not just the General Store. He quickly jumped out of the wagon and headed to the town square.

Once Rucker reached the square, he turned back to see that the boys and the wagon were gone! "Oh no!" he thought. "The boys have left, and they didn't know I was in the wagon! How will I ever find my way home?" Rucker felt scared and began to whimper.

Rucker was sad and thought that he
might never see his family again. Just then he heard a dog
barking from across the street. "Maybe that dog can help me
find my way home," thought Rucker as he ran through the
open gate and toward the house.

Rucker found himself in front of a large house with many white columns and a very unfriendly dog. "I've never seen such a large house before!" exclaimed Rucker. "You don't belong here," growled the dog. "My name is Pug King, and my owner's family founded the town of Roswell. You're a country dog. Go home!" Rucker quickly turned around and ran back out the gate. He would not find anyone here to help him.

Rucker ran back through the town square and across the road. He looked down a long hill and saw a creek lined with mill buildings. He heard men shouting to the mill workers to unload the cotton bales and to keep working. Rucker had never seen this creek or the mill before. He knew this was not the way home. He must keep going and find someone to help him.

Rucker ran down Bulloch Avenue and marveled at the size of the homes with large front porches. His country farmhouse looked nothing like these houses. He was feeling very homesick when he came upon a family playing a game in front of one of the houses. "Maybe they can help me find my way home!" thought Rucker. But the children were no help. "Scat!" they shouted. "Get out of here, country dog!"

Rucker ran down Roswell's main street and past house after house, but no one was at home to help him.

The children at the Academy were having their photograph taken on the school's front steps. They did not have time to help poor Rucker.

Feeling sadder than ever, Rucker continued on and made his way toward Canton Street. The area was lined with shops and businesses. He stopped in front of Mr. Carpenter's wagon and asked his horses, "Do you know where I live?" The horses stamped and snorted in reply, "No, we do not know where you live, country dog, but maybe those men can help you." The horses nodded their heads in the direction of the Perry Building and a group of men standing in front.

Rucker quickly made his way to the group of men and asked, "Do you know where I live?" The men remembered seeing Rucker peeking out from under the burlap sack in the back of the wagon when he came into town. They pointed Rucker in the direction he needed to go. Rucker happily ran on, hoping he would soon be home.

Rucker ran and ran down the road. He was discouraged because he still did not see his home.

Just then, Rucker came upon a large white house with chickens in the front yard. "Do you know where I live?" he asked the chickens. The chickens clucked in reply, "No, we don't, but Mr. Houze lives down that road. He might be able to help you." Rucker barked, "Thank you!" Then he ran toward the house.

Mr. Houze and his dog, Trapper, were sitting outside. Rucker ran up to them and asked, "Do you know where I live?" Trapper barked, "Check with the pigs on Mr. Hembree's farm. They know where everyone lives."

Rucker ran as fast as he could to that
farm. He saw the pigs enjoying their dinner in the barnyard
and asked, "Do you know where I live?" One pig looked up
from his slop and squealed in reply, "Well, your name is
Rucker. Why don't you check with Mr. Rucker? Surely he
will know." And he pointed his corkscrew tail in the right
direction. Rucker was so excited that someone might finally
know how to help him get home. He happily barked all the
way to Mr. Rucker's house.

The whole Rucker family came outside to see what all the commotion was about. Mr. Rucker shouted, "Isn't that Rucker, the Stewart family's dog?" He pointed Rucker to a road that led the way to the Stewart family farm and said, "Go home, Rucker!" Rucker wagged his tail with glee and ran off in the direction of his house.

Rucker ran past all the people in front of the Crabapple store.

He kept running as fast as he could down the road, passing cotton fields and farms along the way. Soon he began to recognize the area around him. He made sure to stay on the road so he did not get lost again. Rucker was thrilled to be going home!

Finally, Rucker came around the bend and saw his farm! He saw his clapboard house, the chickens in his front yard, and his family looking very happy to see him. Mr. Stewart said, "Welcome home, Rucker! Took a little trip into town, did you?" Rucker barked happily in reply, "Roswell was exciting, but I'm so glad I'm just a country dog!"

Acknowledgements

Elaine DeNiro is the archivist for the Roswell Historical Society in Roswell, Georgia. Her love of historic photographs, especially those depicting family pets, led to the discovery of "Rucker" and the writing of the fictional story of his adventure.

Special thanks to Lauren DeNiro Hepper, former teacher and mother of three, who helped shape Rucker's expressive personality.

Connie Huddleston is an historic preservation consultant who specializes in historical research and interpretation. She volunteered to create the book's design.

Gittel Chase Price, who provided our cover photo, is an award-winning photographer, photography teacher, and works to promote women in photography worldwide.

Information about the Images

The historic images found in Rucker, The Lost County Dog are part of the extensive photographic collection housed at the Roswell Historical Society/City of Roswell Research Library and Archives. The locations and people used in this book document life in Roswell, Georgia, around 1900.

"Rucker" really lived about 1900 on a farm outside the City of Roswell with the James Jasper Stewart family.

To learn more, visit www.roswellhistoricalsociety.org

CPSIA information can be obtained
at www.ICGtesting.com
Printed in the USA
LVIW010327170712
290370LV00002B